# AMISS

# AMISS

L. L. McCall

**To order additional copies of this book, contact:**
Xlibris
844-714-8691
www.Xlibris.com
Orders@Xlibris.com
823094

This book is dedicated to my family and friends
who put up with me when I zone out, or sneakily slip away to
write as much as possible.
The late nights when the juices are flowing:
when I must do, what I need to do.
They all put up with me and my craziness,
and I will be forever blessed for it.

# Contents

# Chapter 1

## ~Upside Down~

Unbelievable, Carla thought, as she stood in awe at the edge of the beautiful beachfront property she shared with her husband, Paul, in the tranquil town of Cold Spring Harbor, New York. A slight breeze gently caressed her face as she gazed upon the calm waters and wondered how something could be so beautiful and serene, while there was so much unhappiness in the world. Especially, in her own little corner of the world.

As always, she was mesmerized by the water as it slowly rippled and dashed about with its soft, thin, white foam. The seagulls circled high overhead in the azure sky, as they made their daily routine flight look so effortless. She took a deep breath of the brisk, fresh air. It would soothe her, but only for a little while. Everything just seemed so peaceful and pure compared to her own troubled life, and, yet, for the moment, she felt her life didn't matter at all. Her body felt numb as she wondered how she could go on without her Paul. She'd give anything just to hear his voice once more.

Indeed, Cold Spring Harbor was a very special place. Not only was it rich in wealth, but rich with stories, too. While she had her own personal, riveting story to tell, she really didn't want anyone to know it. She wondered why life couldn't just be simpler, like it used to be. Carla remembered how happy her life had been for so many years, but, it seemed like just a sweet memory now. It was like a jigsaw puzzle, as she struggled to fit all the pieces of her life back together again. The events that led up to this point had twisted and turned her life completely around and upside down. It became too overwhelming for her to think about it anymore, but she had to. She had to go over it in her mind, step-by-step, to make sense of no sense, or it would drive her absolutely insane.

The past seemed so innocent and carefree when she first met the love of her life nearly 11 years ago, when she was 17, going on 18. She lived in a nice, well-to-do area in Woodbury, NY on a very pretty tree-lined street with her Mom, Dad, and older brother, Louis. Their home was a spacious ranch-styled home set on a beautiful acre. It was situated in a popular sought-after neighborhood full of vitality and prosperity, and more importantly, a lot of kids!

It felt like yesterday, as she recalled the morning of June 18, 1981. Carla and several of the kids stood at the bus stop waiting for the bus at their neighborhood's main entrance called, "The Pines." It was right off Main Street where many of the most popular stores were. As they waited, but not so eagerly, they began to feel uncomfortable from the heat already.

Carla was friendly to all of the kids, and always had a smile to give to everyone, but she wasn't as close to any of them as she was to her best friend, Dee who lived a few doors down the block from her. They had known each other since the second grade.

It was only going to be a half day of school, and already she couldn't wait to get it over with. It would've been great if they had no school at all today she felt, but they had to go one more time because of graduation rehearsals. She had her driver's license, but no car. Sometimes her brother would let her borrow his, but he would need it today.

It became a terribly unbearable hot and humid day. The sun showed no mercy. It made Carla and Dee feel somewhat cranky, but they knew after school they would hang out at Izzy's sandwich shop across the street. It was a popular spot, and on days like this they knew the air-conditioning would be blasting. As they stood on their corner and continued to wait for the bus, they stared at Izzy's sign, ready to drool. Just the thought of Izzy's would get them through the day. They were dying just to run in and get anything cold right now, but they couldn't chance missing their bus. They knew they'd be there after school but it couldn't come soon enough. Definitely something to look forward to!

Many times, Carla and Dee would go home with their friends, Joy and Penny, in the neighboring town of Syosset. Joy and Penny lived near some great stores to frequent, too, and a few local fun neighborhood parks. They enjoyed each other's company and liked to just hang out. They could talk for hours on end about anything and everything under the sun. Each day they would plan to go somewhere different, but today with this weather, it was definitely an Izzy's day.

Carla was dressed in one of her favorite summer outfits, a yellow and white-checked gingham cotton jumper. Even though it was a lightweight material, she still felt as if she were still going to melt. She would've rather been in a pool somewhere, or better yet, at the beach. She loved the beach. It was her dream to someday own a home on or near a beach. However, today was definitely not a day for the beach in this sticky heat. It must've been nearly close 91° already!

As the bus came around the corner, everyone sighed. They had a crazy, obnoxious bus driver, Cosmo. Everyone thought he was a lunatic. He wouldn't wait for anyone, even if they were to wave and run behind the bus as they would try to get on. He would laugh, then rant and rave about how they didn't get up early enough. He was somewhat of a speed demon and had all these wacky meters on the bus' dashboard. Maybe it made him feel important, somehow. He would always act like he was in a race! With whom, they didn't know. He would arrive early on purpose to get out as fast as he could from the school's lot. He would master how not to get stuck in the school zone with the crazy parents, as he would put it. He was never late to pick them up, but he was just a bit off the wall!

He arrived at 7:05 am every morning on the dot and school started at 7:35 am and it was only eight minutes away! Just before they were ready to board the bus, Carla took a cute, quick spin with her dress for some air, while she gazed at Izzy's Sandwich Shop sign. She dreaded school on a hot day like today, even if it was for a half day, but the weekend would come soon enough. She would muster up all the energy she could to keep it together and get through this day.

Carla turned to Dee, "One more day of school! I can't wait for tomorrow, our last and final day - forever!"

"You've got that right!" agreed an excited Dee.

As they entered the hot bus, the stench of cashews hit them in the face as Cosmo munched on them. As the bus started to move, Dee took a seat, while Carla threw her bag down on the next seat and opened the bus' window for a breeze of any kind. At that moment, she noticed a very handsome, young man inside Izzy's by the window. Someone she'd never seen before in this small town. He wasn't there moments ago, as they waited for the bus to come, or was he?

Dee noticed him now, too, "Wow, look at that really cute guy sitting in Izzy's," she said.

"Carla, he's looking at you!" Dee blurted, as the young man raised his glass up in the air to Carla, as if to toast her. She cracked a slight smile and could feel herself blush.

# Chapter 2

## ~Daydreaming~

As the bus went down the busy street, Carla's head turned. She couldn't keep her eyes off that certain young man. The young man's glance turned to follow with hers, also. Their eyes were fixed on each other, as her heart raced like never before. It felt like there were 10-pound butterflies in her stomach. She felt flushed and speechless for the moment, which was unusual for her. Cosmo turned the corner, and she wondered if she would ever lay eyes on him again.

"Who was that? I've never seen that guy before. Him, I would have remembered," Carla continued.

"Believe me, if I knew, you would've heard about it already," said Dee. Dee was a little boy crazy. She always knew who was coming and going in this town. And who was with whom.

"Now, I'm going to be curious about who that guy was all day long. I wonder if I will ever see him, again. He was so gorgeous!" Carla rambled on.

"Calm down," said Dee. "He looked too old for you, anyway," as she tried some logic, so Carla wouldn't get her hopes up too much. Carla had just come out of a bad relationship. "Besides, maybe he's only passing through."

"Who cares!" blurted Nan. "I saw him there while we were all at the bus stop. You were both too busy talking about your clothes and how hot it was. He was staring at Carla then!"

Nan always tried to fit in. She wanted to put her two cents in to make them feel stupid. She was a little offbeat, and had had some Carla jealousy issues for many years. Carla never did anything to her on purpose. She was just a pain in the neck, and would always whine about everything.

"I don't believe it! Look! Again, there's another one, walking on the sidewalk towards Izzy's. Wait a minute… twins!" Carla shouted, "This is getting too weird!"

"One for each of us!" boasted Dee.

"Yeah, right! They are both cute, but the more I think about it, I really need to stay focused. I just want to graduate and succeed in college with no ties, except for family and friends. I have no time, or the energy for a new relationship, which will probably end up being a bust like the last loser. Although, when I think about him, he really did look quite outstanding," admitted Carla as she shivered a bit to shake off the thought of him.

"Wow, I saw that shiver as you mentioned him! Very cool - literally!" said Dee as she laughed.

The bus pulled up to the Woodbury high school and the teens got off the bus, but they were in no hurry to get to their classes. As usual, Cosmo got them to school too early.

"Another day of boredom high," exclaimed Dee, as they walked down the hall. Dee didn't care for school, but then again none of them did. She was very bright, yet always seemed elsewhere. Her favorite time of the school day was lunchtime because she loved to socialize. Dee was of an average build at 5'6" with shoulder length dark, wavy hair and large brown, sultry eyes. She had a quick wit, and didn't hold anything back. She had a hard edge to her, so no one messed with her, and by no means, did she ever let anyone take advantage of her. The only ones that ever really saw the soft side of her were her family and Carla.

Soon Carla and Dee met up with their other close friends, Joy and Penny. They had all been close since the seventh grade in junior high school. Meanwhile, Joy and Penny had lived around the corner from each other in nearby Syosset. All the girls would arrive and wait for each other by their lockers every school morning before the first bell. It was their daily ritual. They checked in with each other to make sure they were all there for the day, as best friends would do.

Oh, sure, things weren't always perfect, but for the most part they really did get along great. They loved each other, and when one was unhappy or had a problem, they'd always be there for each other. They knew if something wasn't right among them. They laughed together frequently and cried together occasionally. Even though there were four of them, they knew what the others were thinking - 99.9% of the time!

Today, after they all said their hello's, they grabbed their books and gabbed about the guy they saw in Izzy's. They went on about the other one they saw later that must have been his twin. They would definitely have to get some answers. The class bell rang as they all quickly ran off to where they had to be.

First period came and went, but Carla felt like math class would never end. Thank goodness it was a day with shorter class times. Still, it felt like forever in this heat wave, and, of course, there were no A/C's!

She sat and daydreamed about how she could really fall for this guy. But she felt she had to keep her head screwed on right and not just go on looks. She had to swear off boys so she could concentrate on her future. She had to stop and not think of him, but it was difficult. But, dammit, he was so freaking good looking, as she sighed.

Carla was slender and tall at 5'9" with hazel eyes, and wavy, golden blonde shoulder length hair. Everyone noticed her. She had a certain sparkle about her and a very nice figure. She was a real clothes horse, but not crazy expensive stuff. She always looked nice and put together. Carla had so many aspirations. At times she became too confused over what she wanted to seriously choose. She was very talented and creative, but she had a hard time staying focused, and too often became very easily distracted.

She had high hopes to become a great, beloved artist. You could always see her drawing, or sketching something in a notebook. And it had to be a certain pencil that flowed a certain way when she drew. Whether it was a drawing, a short story, or even just a poem, she would always get back to it eventually to revise or amend it. She hated to leave anything undone. She was a very sensitive, caring person, but worse, she was a crazy romantic, too. She had a lot of interests and would try to figure out how to integrate them all. When it would overwhelm her at times, she would put things aside and put on some music to soothe her. When that didn't help, she would take a long walk.

Carla agonized as she watched the hands on the clock move ever sooooo slowly in her second period Science class. Even though each class was shortened today, they were still so boring. The students just basically sat there and didn't do much of anything. Graduation rehearsals would start shortly afterwards in the gym, and were just as boring, but good for a few laughs. The gym had been all set up with chairs for the big upcoming day. So many kids were happy they didn't have gym for this entire past week.

Finally, thank goodness, the bell rang and school was out for the day. Just one more day and done! It was time to hang out and have some fun! That's all that she could think about, plus, the really cute guy who seeped back into her consciousness. Who was he, she wondered, and should she bother to find out or just forget about him and let it be? Right now, all she could think about was getting something cold to drink!

# Chapter 3

## ~Izzy's~

Happy with the end of the school day, all the girls met at the curb to wait for the bus ride home. They were going to hang out at Izzy's like they've done so many times in the past. Joy and Penny knew the exact spot where to stand, too, as they would all wait for the bus to approach.

Dee said, "Time to get on the darn smelly bus and go!" Today they were on a mission, a "twin mission," to see if they could get any information out of Wanda, the cashier at Izzy's. Were there really two of them? It had to have been. Both Carla and Dee had seen them!

"If anybody would know about those guys, it would be Wanda. She would have the entire scoop," said Penny.

"Oh, Penny, I'm not looking to get involved with anyone now. I really should have my head examined," said Carla.

Then Carla began to question herself. What am I doing? I know I really shouldn't pursue a relationship, but I can't help it, she thought. Her curiosity would get the better of her. Her mind was saying one thing, but her heart was saying another. None of them would rest until they got some answers. Then all of a sudden, Carla remembered his beautiful smile, and her heart skipped a beat. She had never felt like this. Oh sure, she'd had boyfriends in the past, but there was something undeniably different about him, at least, from first impressions.

Wanda was a sweet woman in her early 60's. She was a feisty lady and a great listener, too. Carla could never forget how when a few years back, a couple of teenagers tried to skip out on their bill. She had run down the block after them and brought them back by their ears! She made them scrub all the dirty dishes, not once, but twice. What a sight that was! Dee and Carla were so hysterical with laughter when it happened that they almost peed in their pants. Wanda had been at Izzy's since, well, since forever! Since time started, the girls would kid about! They couldn't wait to see Wanda and grill her!

On the bus ride home, all they could talk about was trying to find out who the handsome, young guys were. They thought about who may have had relatives in from out of town that came in for a visit. But twins were never brought up in conversation, as far as they can remember. Everyone pretty much knew each other in this town, and their curiosity had been peaked all day, (especially Carla's)!

As they got off the bus stop at the corner, the girls crossed over to Izzy's. Nonchalantly, they saunter in as if the so-called twins might still be there. But, of course, they weren't. Too much time had passed. But they didn't worry. They were thirsty, and the air conditioning was just absolute bliss. They said their "hellos" to Wanda and Gus, the cook. Dee and Carla planned to linger about at the front register by Wanda, as they had to wait patiently for a customer to leave after they paid their tab.

Gus, on the other hand, was a really funny guy in his late 60's with a heavy Greek accent who loved to cook. He had a passion for it since he'd been a little boy growing up in Greece. He always gave the girls' new dishes to sample. They frequented the place the most, it seemed.

His gray hair made him look so distinguished, but his belly was another story, especially once he came out from behind the counter. He would treat all the girls' with respect and he was like a father figure to them. He looked out for them and had known them since they had been little when they came in with their parents. It was their happy place, a nice family spot decorated with a 50's vibe with a lot of turquoise, red, and white colors.

While Joy and Penny piled into their favorite booth, they would play a few songs on the player. Carla and Dee continued to hang out up front near Wanda. They had to wait as a few more customers came up to pay their tabs, and leave. Oh, the torture!

In the meantime, Stella, their favorite waitress, went over to the booth to take orders from Joy and Penny, who only wanted soda floats with ice cream. Stella was a natural beauty, in her mid 30's, and originally from Georgia. She had no family nearby, but Gus and Wanda were like family to her. She was a terrific waitress, and never screwed up anyone's order, either. Sometimes when she thought Gus wasn't looking, she'd give the girls extra scoops of ice cream; but he saw, and he loved her for it.

"Oh, Joy sugar," Stella said in her southern drawl as she leaned over to place some more napkins in their holder, "there was a young fellow in here earlier asking a lot of questions about Carla." She described the young man, and Joy and Penny went ballistic. Carla and Dee were still by Wanda at the front counter. They heard Joy and Penny making a commotion at the back of the diner.

"Carla!" Penny shouted, and the whole place fell silent as she slumped back into the booth from embarrassment. She didn't mean to scare anyone; she was just excited for Carla, of course.

Carla gasped as she turned around quickly. Joy and Penny were flailing their arms like lunatics as they waved for her to come back there. Dee and Carla rushed back to the booth to find out why they were acting so unhinged.

"What's the matter? What's wrong?" Carla asked. Penny had been going so nuts that the entire table was shaking.

Dee asked, "What the heck has gotten into you?"

"Sit, sit!" said Joy.

"You're not going to believe this!" said Penny.

"What? Tell me!" said Carla.

"When Stella took our orders, she didn't realize you were here. She said there was a young man in here earlier that asked about the girl with the blonde hair at the bus stop earlier this morning? Stella realized he meant you, Carla," said Penny.

When Stella arrived with their orders, Carla's heart raced with excitement. She gently grabbed Stella by the arm and would not let her go until she had her every question answered.

"Stella, what did you say, who is he, where is he from, why me?" Carla rambled. For someone who didn't want to get involved, she really became interested now.

"He just thought you were the prettiest thing he ever did see," Stella said. "I just told him you were one of the local high school girls, and that your name was Carla."

"That's it? What about his name? What else did he say? Who is his family? Where do they live? Is he here just visiting? Are there two of them?" Carla's questions tumbled out. She tried to contain herself, with no success.

Stella replied, "Calm down, honey-girl. He'll be back later tonight at 7 o'clock and I was to tell you, if I saw you. I told him you were always in here, but not so much on a school weeknight, but that you were here more often right after school and on the weekends. He felt if you didn't show, he would think that you weren't interested, so I had to tell him weekends were better, so he'd understand. He would still come by tonight, to take a chance you might show up. He's a real pretty boy, too! He has black gorgeous, thick hair with the bluest of blue eyes. He said his name is Paul, and then just about five minutes later, his twin brother walked in. His name is Peter, and you really can't tell them apart." Then Stella was called away by Gus' ringing bell.

"Wow, so we're coming back?" Joy asked. Joy was the serious one and very smart, not just book smart, but street smart, also. She was tall about 5'7" with dark blonde, long, straight hair and pretty blue almond-shaped eyes. Sometimes you didn't know she was around because she was quiet, but if she had something to say, she'd say it. She was too smart for her own good, but she knew what she wanted and behaved like she had total control over her life. She had a wonderful dry sense of humor and was very down to earth. She always had a great comeback if anyone annoyed her, and Carla loved her for that.

"You think I should? No, I can't. It'll make me look too forward," said Carla, not being able to think straight, as they all looked at her intensely and waited for an immediate answer. Carla tried so hard to be aloof and to pretend not to care. But they could see it in her face as she grappled with the idea of it. She believed she'd be nuts not to go for it. But now the nerves had kicked in, and her stomach took over.

"Oh, I can't, I just can't bring myself to show up, and we have the last day of school tomorrow," said Carla as she turned to Dee, "What do you think, Dee?"

"You should just go for it. It couldn't hurt, and you might really like this guy, and we'll all be right here for you," said Dee.

"Yeah, Carla, we can arrive here early, and then you walk in by yourself, as if you're here to meet us. Maybe he'll be already here," said Penny.

"Make a grand entrance, all decked out, then come and sit with us. What's there to think about?" said Joy, being supportive.

"You have to do this. I've never, ever seen you act like this before. This could the best thing that's happened to you in while. You deserve it, Carla. If you don't then you'll wonder what could have been, and maybe never see this guy again. Forget about all those jokers in the past. This guy just may be the one," said Penny.

Penny was a risk-taker at 5'8" with gorgeous, straight, thick red hair and warm brown/hazel eyes, with a great determination to whatever she put her mind to. She was really book smart, loved to write, and play guitar. She had a great mind and was very business savvy, too. She was outspoken almost as much as Dee.

"You're not going to let a chance like this slip away, are you?" asked Dee. "Forget about what your brain says and do what your heart feels!"

"All right, all right, I'll do it, but I'm warning you guys, you better not make me feel silly. I'm getting nervous already just thinking about it," said Carla.

# Chapter 4

## ~Heart On The Line~

As the appointed hour closely approached, Carla chose something really sweet and simple to wear. She didn't want to appear too forward or racy. She was very excited, but nervous, too. She told her parents she was meeting Dee at Izzy's and wouldn't be too late. Everything was fine so far, except her stomach. As she tried to relax she would convince herself that he was just another typical guy out for a good time. It would help her to get turned off so she could move on. Besides, he could be just a total jerk and full of himself because of his looks.

She would downplay it as much as she could. She literally tried to talk herself out of feeling anything for this guy, but she didn't really succeed. The vision of him when he lifted his glass to her played out over and over in her head. If only her stomach would calm down. She felt queasy the more she thought about him. Carla just wanted to get through the night. Then she ran to the bathroom and threw up...

It was soon time to go. Carla somewhat settled down and gained some composure. She felt a little bit shaky after she got off the phone with Dee. They had confirmed their appointed time, and that they would go through with it, come hell or high water. The plan was that Carla would walk into Izzy's precisely at 7:08 pm on the dot. They would all set their watches as it came close to the zero hour.

"Oh, my God, I can't believe this guy has got me turned upside down and inside out for that matter," she said. "And I haven't even met him yet! I've got to stop thinking so hard and forget his face, at least until I actually do see him. Oh my," she worried. "What if I puke in front of him?" and then she ran into the bathroom to throw up some more. She didn't think she had anything left!

All of a sudden there was a knock on the bathroom door, and it was her older brother, Louis. "Hey, muscles, you almost done in there, or do you need more time to talk to yourself?" 'Muscles,' was the nickname he and his boyhood friends called her back in the day, because when they bothered her, she'd hit them. Louis was only two years older and bossed her around a lot, but he was getting better with age.

"Go away, use the other bathroom!" Carla shouted. She freshened up her makeup, while under much duress. As she watched the time carefully, she finally ventured out. She decided it was something she needed to do, so she wouldn't have to wonder about what could have been.

"Let's do this," she encouraged herself. It was still light out, so she would walk. It was close enough and she felt calm knowing her friends were already there. It gave her a much-needed boost of confidence and courage. The evening air was still humid, but a slight breeze made it more bearable. The stores were brightly lit and clear. The smell of the summer night air relaxed her as she heard some male crickets singing to attract their mates. It was a sound she liked to fall asleep to, but was she a cricket tonight? She smiled and giggled, as she thought about that.

She continued on her walk, passed a few neighbors outside their homes and waved. Almost there, she began to see the sidewalk shops bustling with young parents, kids licking their ice cream cones, and older kids playing kickball in the adjacent park. Men were smoking their big, fat cigars and hanging out on the benches and stoops, laughing and retelling their old stories. She waved hello nervously to all the ones that she knew. Now she had only one agenda tonight, and that was to get through it.

She still couldn't believe what she was doing. As she stuck to the plan, she would grab the door at Izzy's at the precise time of 7:08 pm. All of the craziness was going through her mind as she tried to rationalize and calm herself as she approached the door! Carla was about to pull it open, then all of a sudden, a hot flash came over her. I can't believe it I've never felt like this, she thought. This is so incredibly insane; I really have to get my act together. She hesitated for a moment, and considered going back home. Too late, her friends already saw her and waved her in. Now I'm stuck, she thought. She walked in towards them with her eyes only on the girls and not allowing herself to look anywhere else. She pretended that she didn't know he would be there and would put on a surprise act if he was.

It didn't matter. He wasn't. Wanda mentioned he wasn't there. Everyone knew and what may or may not happen. She felt a tremendous relief. Her stomach didn't hurt as much anymore. She still couldn't bring herself to look up to check it out for herself. She would then look for Dee and sat in the booth with her friends.

"Whoops, Wanda spoke too soon; he just walked in, Carla," Dee said.

"So much for the grand entrance," giggled Joy.

"Oh, I can't believe my nerves," said Carla.

"Relax, he's only the most gorgeous guy you'd ever want to meet!" said Penny.

"Thanks! That makes my stomach feel so much better now!" she exclaimed.

He sat up at the front counter and ordered a soda. It looked like he was about to order something more, but then he looked around and spotted her. He pointed to the back where Carla and the girls sat. Carla saw all of this as he turned to look at her. Their eyes met, and there wasn't another soul around. For a moment, she couldn't breathe and she was rendered still. As noisy and busy as it was, you just couldn't break through the force that was going on between them. She felt warm and energized all over, but with a calm and gentle peace at the same time. It was one of the greatest feelings she had ever felt. She knew and felt immediately he was very special. Her butterflies had butterflies!

He got up and began to walk over to her. Even his eyes smiled. She sighed quietly and slightly melted a bit. He extended his hand to her, as he introduced himself.

"Hello, my name is Paul. I'm new to the area," he said.

"Hi," is all she could muster up. (Oh, what a stupid, stupid hello, she thought, so she tried to sound more intelligent. She tried so hard to form words from her mouth, but her brain was on a mini vacation).

"I live around here," she said, (oh, no - again, how stupid, she thought).

"I know, I asked that nice waitress over there, and she told me a little about you. May I buy you a soda?" he asked.

The girls just watched the goings-on back-and-forth, as their heads went back and forth with their conversation. They would practically push Carla out of the booth.

"Go on, Carla, we can spare you," Penny laughed.

"Oh, where are my manners," said Carla. "This is Joy, Penny, and

Dee, my longtime friends," as she pointed to each of them. All of them smiled at him and gave little waves of hello.

"Nice to meet you all," as Paul reached out for Carla's hand. His touch made her feel so alive and off they went to be alone in another booth so they could get to know each other.

Her stomach settled down some as she sipped her soda slowly. It actually helped settle her stomach. She had begun to feel very comfortable with him. He was so courteous and very pleasant, and he wasn't bad to look at, either. She began to laugh, and you could see she was really having a great time. The minutes just flew by, and turned into hours as time stood still for them. Customers would come and go and they didn't even notice. It seemed like they had so much to talk about. She learned more about him in this short amount of time than she had ever known about anybody else, except maybe her closest friends, of course. It was strange, though. She felt as if she had known him forever as she got lost in his beautiful, blue eyes.

Her friends soon became antsy and wanted to leave, as it became very late for a school night. They needed to get home with one day left of school. Then graduation would be just two days away on Sunday. Although, they were the last ones to leave, they were excited for Carla. They wouldn't leave her alone with him, but they didn't want to interrupt them, either, but they had to. It was getting near 11pm, and they didn't want the parents to send out any S.O.S.'s. Their parents knew the phone number at Izzy's all too well, and the girls didn't want to get embarrassed. They walked over and asked how things were and asked Carla if she was ready to leave.

"Can I have your phone number to call you, Carla?" Paul asked.

"All right," Carla sweetly replied, as she wrote down her phone number on a nearby napkin. She was definitely attracted to this guy, as he was clearly interested in her. They both sensed it right away. Carla felt she was destined to be with him, but should she get her hopes up too high just yet? Maybe, it was too good to be true! He offered to give her a ride home, but she stayed with her plan to walk home with Dee instead. (It was fine, she didn't want her parents to see him drop her off - not yet).

# Chapter 5

## *~Inseparable~*

Graduation day came and it was a blast! Although, all she could think about was Paul. Her parents with her brother took her out for a nice celebratory dinner at their local favorite Italian restaurant, Mangia's. It was decorated with beautiful paintings of Italian scenery throughout, even in the halls to the bathrooms. But, more importantly, she couldn't wait to run to Izzy's to meet Paul afterwards.

After a few short weeks, Carla and Paul became very close, and they couldn't help the way they felt about each other. One night they decided to go for a walk in the local park. It was such a clear, beautiful night with the sky filled with so many brilliant stars. They just had to sit on the bench and enjoy it.

"Wow, I can't believe how close the stars feel. It's just so incredible how beautiful they look," said Carla.

"They are beautiful, but they can't compare to you, my sweetness," said Paul, as he looked at her, he leaned in to kiss her. The kisses became passionate, but it certainly wasn't the right place.

He continued to hold her then told her, "I really do love you, and I can't take it not being able to be alone with you, but I will remain patient," he said. She knew what he meant and how he felt. She had had other boyfriends before, but she was still a virgin. She was embarrassed to say anything about it to Paul, and it made her uncomfortable. She felt she was too inexperienced for him, but when the time and place were right, they'd both know.

For now, they would take it slow. He had just turned 20 in May, and she would be 18 in August, but things would not slow down too much for these two. It came to the point where if you saw Carla, you'd see Paul, too. The same if you saw Paul, you'd see Carla. They went everywhere together; the movies, the mall, bowling, dining, local stores, the beach, the park. You name it. They did it. They were completely inseparable.

Paul never really talked too much about his twin brother, Peter. He was just so enamored with Carla. He told her that Peter traveled a lot, and was not around much. She would get to meet him soon enough.

Paul's family was having a get-together for the 4th of July at his parent's house in the neighboring area across Main Street in another part of Woodbury. He wanted her to come and finally meet the entire family. July 4th was around the corner.

With all the hoopla, pomp, and circumstance the 4th of July could only bring, Paul and Carla were definitely excited to share their very first one together today! Carla hurried to get ready, and Paul would be there shortly to pick her up. On his way out, Paul ran into Peter who had just arrived home.

"Hey bro, where are you running off to? I just got here!" said Peter.

"I have to leave to get Carla, and you're going to love her. I can't wait for you to meet her! And you'd better be really nice to her, because she's the one!" Paul exclaimed. "And, take a shower - you kinda stink!"

"Yeah, yeah, it's just like old times, already... telling me what to do," Peter responded with a chuckle.

"Well, it great to see you, too! Hey! We have a lot of catching up to do! I'll be back real soon!" said Paul, "And be on your best behavior!"

As Carla got into Paul's' car, he told her how excited he was that his brother had just come home, and he couldn't wait to introduce them. He warned Carla that Peter was a bit of a ladies' man, but told her not to worry and, hopefully, he'd behave. As Paul arrived at the house with Carla, they found Peter on the family room sofa with only a robe on. His hair was wet as he strummed on his beat-up guitar.

"Hi Peter, nice to meet you," Carla said with a sweet smile.

"You, too, I heard a lot about you" Peter said without even getting up. (Right away she saw he had zero manners).

"Well, I hope it's all good?" she replied.

"Nah, actually... No, no, I'm just kidding," Peter continued and laughed. He could see how Paul was really taken with her; just by the way his brother looked at her.

He was arrogant, she thought. Her gut reaction was that she didn't care for him, but out of respect for Paul she'd put on a nice smile, and would give him a chance. It was unbelievable how much they looked exactly alike, she felt.

Carla and Paul walked into the kitchen to say hello to his parents, Mr. and Mrs. Thompson. They were very sweet to Carla. They insisted she call them Pat and Mike, and were delighted to see Paul was very happy.

Most of the festivities were in the backyard. There were cousins, aunts, uncles, and a few neighbors all over the place. At first, she was a bit overwhelmed but it was a lot of fun to meet everyone.

Unfortunately, as the day went on, things went a little bit downhill. Peter continued to brag about this girl, that girl, and to suggest that Paul come with him next time to these wild, exotic places, right in front of Carla. It bothered her, but she laughed it off.

Paul answered that he couldn't be bothered. He had already found what he had been looking for as he gazed at Carla, and put Peter in his place. He was a very determined, young man and felt he wanted to declare his complete and undying love for Carla. He believed she felt the same.

Weeks turned into months as they became so close that she hardly saw her friends, anymore. They missed her and she missed them, but she was intoxicated by this incredible new love.

Dee would always call Carla, but she was never home. When she was, she was just about to go out the door to meet Paul. It became so bad that one day she ran into her and cornered her at a local store. They agreed to set one day aside to get together. A friend's day, and they'd stick by it. Every Thursday afternoon would be their special day, no matter what! It worked for a several weeks, but eventually it faded away.

Joy went to Cornell University to study veterinary sciences. Dee helped out at Izzy's as a waitress, and Penny got a job at a local attorney's office in nearby Plainview, while studying to be a paralegal. She would need to work to pay for her own studies, but she loved it. Eventually her goal would be to go into the city to work at a big law firm. In the meantime, Carla studied fashion design at a small local college, and one day would hope to open her own little dress and accessory shop. But, for now, all her free time was spent with Paul. She studied hard on campus, and loved her classes, but when she came home, she was all his.

Paul had a promising career at a local bank and started to make very good money. He planned to sock it away. After all, he wanted to marry Carla and build a life with her. His father was very successful in the finance world. His Dad's great ethics had rubbed off on him, as he admired and paid very close attention to his Dad's example over the years. As for his twin, Peter, who had no interest in getting a job, who would continue to play music gigs from town to town, here and there. No more fancy trips for a while, but he still felt he was going to find his pie-in-the-sky with music! It was his dream and he loved the lifestyle that went along with it. No matter how often he would have his bubble burst, he never gave up. At least, he had determination in something.

Paul and Carla began to entertain talk about marriage. It scared her, but she knew, without a doubt, he was the one. No one else ever made her feel the way he did. She was head over heels for him. They agreed to wait until she had at least two years of college under her belt, and that's what they did. It wasn't an easy wait, but he was very patient and loyal. In the meantime, he would focus on building a future and solid nest egg for both of them.

He applied to a local brokerage firm to become a stockbroker as he learned "the ropes." As a trainee, he planned on taking his series 7 exam very soon. He was a natural and his new boss really liked him. He was a hard worker, was never late, had a great attitude, and was a great team player. The boss saw a lot of potential in him.

His twin, Peter, on the other hand, was a real slacker and he acted like everybody owed him. He hung out mostly with his friends just to waste time at the beach, or off once again on his local travels, gig after gig, just really going everywhere, but really getting nowhere.

Paul soon became a full-fledged stockbroker and soon after a wealth management advisor. While Carla studied, he worked himself up the ladder after several, long tedious and hard years. Carla always encouraged him and was thrilled he was happy and successful, which made her happy! One of the partners, Mr. Cole, of the brokerage firm had taken him under his wing early on, and soon Paul became his right-hand man and confidant. He began to do so well with the investments that the money was literally rolling in for him and his client base. He was a shoo-in for a big promotion soon.

Carla graduated college with honors and started her own little specialized design shop from home until it got too big. She opened a brick-and-mortar store downtown, and she just loved it. She started to do well and built a nice clientele base. She was able to hire a few sales people and the shop ran smoothly. Paul dazzled and showered her with everything and anything that she could possibly want. He loved showering her with attention. They had great careers and felt beyond blessed.

One night he planned a beautiful romantic dinner at their favorite Italian restaurant. He wanted to propose, but was too nervous that she might say it was too soon. Yet, he chose a beautiful, round diamond ring and decided to take the chance. He had asked Stella to help contact all the girls so they could be there for this special event. He wanted everything to be perfect with both sides of the family there, too.

He planned to propose at Mangia's because it was the perfect spot with enough space to accommodate everybody. It had become one of their special places over the past few years. Paul had considered about doing it at Izzy's, where they had met, but he wanted the setting to be upscale and more romantic.

Days later, his plan came together as he and Carla entered the restaurant. Everyone hid in the backroom waiting on pins and needles! As Paul and Carla were seated at their favorite table in the dimly-lit corner, their guests waited in silence as he began his speech.

"Here, let me help you with that," as he reached over to help her off with her sweater. While they sat, Paul started to sweat.

She looked at him, "Are you okay?"

He nervously replied, "I'm better than okay, I'm great!"

"What does that mean?" she asked concerned, "Are you sure you're okay?"

He said, "I can't wait any longer," then he stood up and got down on one knee.

"Oh my God," she gasped, and then looked around to see who was watching as she saw family and friends come into the room to bear witness to his plan.

Her hands over her mouth, she was in complete and utter shock as he continued with his proposal.

"Carla, ever since I laid eyes on you, I knew you were the one. You are an incredible, loving, and sweet person. Never in my life have I ever felt so connected with someone that made me feel so happy every day. All I do is think about you in every waking moment, and when I'm not with you, it drives me crazy. I would be honored to have you as my wife to love and cherish you forever. You are the light of my life, and I love you so much. I am so grateful that fate has brought us together. Will you marry me?"

Tears rolled down her reddened cheeks, as she nodded her head up and down and said, "Yes, of course, I will, and I love you, too."

After he slipped the ring on her finger, they embraced, accompanied by screams and cheers as people clapped everywhere. Even other patrons, who they didn't know, joined in. Family and friends came over to offer hugs with well wishes and congratulations.

Unfortunately, Peter was a no-show for a while. In typical fashion, he would show up later on for the free drinks.

Life seemed so phenomenal for Paul and Carla. A few months later they had a gorgeous, yet, small wedding at a home he rented on the water. Not too lavish, but still it was like a dream come true for Carla to get married to the love of her life.

Peter on the other hand, although, he tried to wear a brave face, couldn't hold it together so he ended up leaving the reception early. He was happy for them but it was bittersweet at the same time. He was exhausted from all the fluctuation of feelings coming over him. He wanted to be like his brother so much that he became resentful.

In the meantime, Paul made arrangements to buy the beautiful home they got married at as a surprise wedding gift. It was on a beachfront two-acre property in Cold Spring Harbor, NY. It was absolutely breathtaking. He made all her dreams come true, and she couldn't be happier. Everything just fell into place for them and they felt life was so perfect. But really, was it?

# Chapter 6

## ~Boredom Setting In~

His parents adored Carla, as hers did Paul. However, on the other hand, her older brother, Louis, didn't care about any of it. Oh, sure he was happy that his sister was happy, but he did his own thing. He met a girl named Victoria and would eventually move upstate near Poughkeepsie. And, of course, Carla was thrilled for him, too, but he was another one who was in his own world, just like Peter.

Paul and his family used to live in New York City, before they came to Woodbury. Mr. and Mrs. Thompson had felt they wanted a more suburban simpler life, and were glad to be here for these past few years. Mr. Thompson had wanted to semi-retire, anyway, and he was thrilled he took the leap. It was his chance to slow down when he accepted an offer to be an advisor for a local firm in Melville. Besides, as a family, they all needed a change and it certainly had changed Paul's life forever, as he'd met the love of his life.

Growing up, Paul was always easy going, but Peter was a handful, as their parents and housekeeper, Joanna, would attest to. Peter and Paul were such opposites like Jekyll and Hyde. As they grew, their mom always thought it was interesting to see how they interacted with each other. Every day was a new adventure, especially when they started school. Mrs. Thompson always thought they balanced each other. Peter, at an early age, was a smooth talker and always seemed to get out of anything. Of course, as he got older, it didn't change.

Paul on the other hand, was always such a good kid, and was a star pupil. He always looked out for his twin brother. When Peter got in trouble, Paul would stick up for him, and would occasionally take the blame for him.

As Paul and Carla got settled into married life, they both had their plates full at work. Paul became less attentive to Carla, so she busied herself with the shop more. She loved to keep busy and was so creative, but she didn't need to work. Her job didn't feel like a job, and it made her feel fulfilled. From time to time her friends would come into the shop, and they would go for a quick lunch to catch up. When they were younger, the girls were inseparable, but things changed as they got older which made her a bit sad. However, she was grateful for any time she could spend with them.

Home alone in their big house, she felt lonely a lot of the time. Although, Joanna, the housekeeper, was around most of the time, it just wasn't the same. When Paul's parents went down to Florida for a few months, Joanna would work for Paul and Carla. It worked out nicely for Joanna who liked the change. She wanted to stay in NY full-time, because her own family was here, too.

It had been some time since anyone had heard from Peter. It was probably a good thing. It meant he was busy and he told everyone he had been traveling around with a well-established band. Paul adored his brother, and seemed blind to his flaws. Paul felt everyone else just misunderstood Peter, but he knew his brother had talent, too. Peter was now finding some success, or at least, that's what he told everyone.

Carla's business was doing very well, but she needed some alone time once in a while. She had three trustworthy employees to help run the shop when she needed a reprieve.

Carla spent more time around the house and became a little bored until she picked up her paints again. She painted some beautiful paintings and over time she gave quite a few away as presents. Only a few were very special to her, and those she kept. For some reason, it still didn't fulfill her enough. She would go into the shop every few days, but it didn't feel like it used to. For her, the thrill of the challenge was gone.

She wanted more, but didn't know of what. She and Paul began to have different interests. She tried to busy herself with projects, and he worked late more and more. She loved the shop, but it began to stress her out, too. She would decorate and rearrange furniture in the house, and then go on to refurbish the pool house and cottage on the back property. She found a whole new interest in decorating.

One uneventful day, Peter showed up at the door, and asked if he could hang out for a while until his next gig. No one knew exactly what that meant, but then neither did he. There really was no next gig. He had been thrown out of the last motel for boozing it up, and then tried to dodge the place without paying for his exorbitant bill. He looked haggard, but Carla couldn't turn him away. He was the twin of the love of her life. She let him use the shower and borrow some of Paul's clothes.

Paul came home to find Peter was all spruced up. Peter was clean-shaven and looked great as Paul welcomed him without any hesitation.

"Hey, bro, you're looking sharp!" as Paul laughed.

"Thanks, bro, you got good taste!" Peter replied.

They relaxed in the family room and began to reminisce while they laughed and had a few beers. Carla would retire early leaving them to reconnect, only to later on hear Peter as he played on his guitar and sang. She thought he sounded so beautiful and full. She was really in shock. She had never bothered to hear him perform anywhere, because it was mostly in different states. He always wanted to leave and travel. Maybe he really did find his niche' and was just unlucky in finding the right connections. With all those years as he tried to make it, at least practice appeared to make perfect.

The next morning at the breakfast table, Carla told him how wonderful he sounded. Paul had gone to work already and left Peter a note that said he would be home early and hang out with him later.

"I would love to show you some of my old poems, and maybe you can make some songs out of them. I have them just sitting in a drawer," said Carla.

He smiled, "Yeah, that'd be cool," just being polite. He then took off and said, "I'll see ya later!"

She went upstairs and dug them out and planned to show them to Peter later. When he came back, she asked him to look at them. He didn't seem interested at first, but he had a complete turnaround and liked quite a few of them. All of a sudden, they had camaraderie. She felt someone could finally appreciate her written words, and he actually thought they were really, really good.

She never mentioned them to Paul, as she wasn't sure they were good enough. They were just stuffed in a dresser drawer for so many years from when she was younger, and had brought them with her when they moved. They were like her secret jewels hidden away to one day to be taken out on a rare occasion when she felt an urge to reminisce, or show someone who might appreciate them.

That evening Peter had a heart to heart with Paul and told him the truth about being out of a job, and asked if he could possibly work the grounds for room and board until he found a real job. The music scene just wasn't cutting it for him anymore, especially as he was getting older. He'd had a few good years, but felt it was time to move on to something else more stable. Maybe Paul could recommend something for him.

Paul couldn't say no to his brother. He knew it hadn't been easy for him, although, he didn't agree with his lifestyle, either. However, he insisted that he stay and that he would pay him a salary to do odd jobs around the place. Not that it needed much of anything because it was so beautiful to begin with, but he told him not to worry. He could stay as long as he wanted and to help himself to anything he wanted.

Weeks went by and before long he tried to help himself to Carla. She thought, at first, he was just being clumsy. The problem was that Peter hung around in the house so much that it became very uncomfortable. While Paul was so focused and too consumed with work, he was clueless when it came to his brother's intentions. He trusted him and would never think twice about him being around Carla like that. It was his brother and he felt Peter knew and understood how he felt about his Carla. Isn't that what twins feel and sense about each other? They had a special connection, a bond of trust, right? Paul always felt he was in tune with his brother. He would never acknowledge that Peter was so narcissistic.

# Chapter 7

## ~Success Breeds Success~

Like so many couples, Paul and Carla had many similar interests, but just as many different interests, too. But it was all good, as it made for interesting conversation at the dinner table many a night. She still loved Paul very much, but she felt Paul loved his work more than her lately. They certainly weren't newlyweds anymore. She became lonely, and Peter continued to show an incredible amount of interest in her writings… and her.

While Peter now lived in the cottage on the back of the property, he became way too comfy in the main house, also. When Paul took him on as an additional groundskeeper, they hadn't really needed one. Nestor, their regular guy, was already terrific. So now Peter would boss Nestor around to do all the work and then take credit for it. The refurbished cottage Peter lived in was set up as a guest house for when family and friends came to visit. Now Peter was the family guest that wouldn't leave. Peter told Paul that he loved working for him but in reality, he hated playing second fiddle to his successful brother.

His attraction to Carla became stronger and he started to get more "handsy" with her. She didn't forget about his reputation of being a ladies' man and he still remained full of himself. While she didn't care for it, she liked his confidence and the undeniable attention. He was full of life, unlike Paul who buried his nose in paperwork, and had become kind of a bore. She tried to get the spark back with Paul, but he was always too exhausted when he got home. Nonetheless, she had to try to ignore Peter as best she could.

She would never leave her husband to be with Peter. It was absurd! While the looks were there, but that was it! She loved her husband very much. When she had her doubts, she would often remind herself how she had met Paul, and how it all began for them years ago. The connection they had and how she had fallen so hard for him back then. They had had a whirlwind romance, and it was very special. Now she questioned whether it was over, but in her heart, she truly felt the answer was, no. Life would just continue to take them on a journey!

While Peter and Carla began to see more and more of each other around the house, she felt she had to busy herself outside of the house more often. His advances became too intense. He made himself available for her too much. He became overly obvious, and she couldn't let herself get caught up in it. When Joanna was around, he would back down. At times, it was a challenge, and while she missed her husband's attention, she had needs, too.

One afternoon Peter went too far, and he became a little too familiar as he grabbed and kissed her.

"I know you want it" Peter said.

"I cannot believe you! Your own brother's wife!" she pushed him away and stormed out of the room.

Paul arrived home tired from a long day at work and sensed her frustration with Peter around the house. At dinnertime, Paul discussed with Peter how things were going great for him at his job. He wanted to create some interest in Peter. Paul suggested that Peter come with him to his office the next day. He would loan him a nice suit, and one day take him to buy a few more.

Paul figured if he was anything like him at all, maybe he would take to it. I mean, who didn't like money, Paul thought. Especially since their own father was so successful.

The next day Peter went with Paul to work all dressed up and it was impossible to tell the difference between the two of them. After they parked in Paul's private spot, together, they approached the front glass double-doors.

"This is it, bro," said Paul, as he stood before the building with his arm around his brother's shoulders.

"It's a big place, but before you know it - you can be up there with the best of them," continued Paul with a big smile.

"Wow, this place is huge, I had no idea," said Peter.

"I've got to get you out more often! You'll get used to it," said Paul. "This is my second home away from home," he continued.

Although, Peter already knew that, he was definitely impressed. It was a nice modern three-story building in the Jericho Metro area. Paul was very proud of himself, and it showed. Peter's crazy lifestyle as a freeloader had hopefully caught up to him. Paul had hoped he would take this step seriously, (while literally), they continued on their journey up the large steps into the building. While Paul just wanted to encourage his brother, and hoped to put an end to his 'dreaming,' he still went all out for him. When Peter saw his brother's name, "Paul Thompson," in the lobby's directory, he felt very envious.

Paul had made him feel totally welcomed at home and now at the office. He would want his brother to be as happy and successful as he was. He introduced him to many of the staff and, of course, they all couldn't believe how much they looked exactly alike. Together they walked around the office then into Paul's elaborate, but messy office.

"I can help you study and ace that exam. I can train you with the best in the business, and I'll always be around to help. What do you think?" asked Paul.

"Are you sure you want to waste your time on me?" asked Peter.

"Oh, you're such a jerk! Why do you say something like that? One day we'll open our own and it'll be called the 'Thompson Brother's Brokerage,' but I'm not going to let you get off that easy, you're going have to work hard for it!" said Paul. "So what? You got a late start. You tried the music thing, but now it's time to get serious!" Peter didn't care for that remark, but he managed a smile.

Peter really couldn't care less. Although, he was definitely tempted, he would always find some excuse to bail on his brother sooner or later. As usual, he just wanted everything for nothing. He wanted what Paul had, but without doing the work. He reported to the job with him for the next few months, but, unfortunately, he tried to slide by doing as little as possible. He wasn't so great around the house grounds, either. He was an office flirt. Annoyed, Paul excused it, feeling it was a sign of Peter's deep-down insecure personality. Peter had shown minimal interest in the work, but more interest in a few women which gave him a reason to return to the office.

Soon Paul needed to get prepared for an upcoming two-week business trip, visiting several cities in that set time. He would have back-to-back conferences and meetings with other large firms and big investors. Although, he wanted Carla to come with him, he knew he would have little to no down time, and she would be bored out of her mind. Next time he would take her with him and where there would be more places to visit and enjoy. The faster he got this one out of the way, the faster he could get home to her, and take some time off to make some special future plans. Even as he was preparing to leave the next day, his only thought was about how soon he would return home.

In the meantime, Carla had plenty of things to do. Her focus was to finish a very special water view painting she had begun. She escaped to the backyard for several afternoons in the gorgeous summer weather. It kept her mind open and free and provided much needed alone time. It was her little mini vacation, just to hear the water gently splash against the rocks, feel the breeze, and enjoy all the different birds as they sang.

She had a great set-up and kept her materials very organized. It was such a labor of love. When she went to take a break, she walked back towards the house to get something refreshing to drink. Joanna was out shopping, and she was surprised to see Peter rummaging through the refrigerator. He should have been at the office while Paul was away, but, true to Peter's character, he took advantage of the boss. How Paul could let him get away with this was beyond imagination, Carla thought. Obviously, he didn't know his brother as well as he thought.

"What are you doing here?" asked a surprised Carla.

"I ran out of cold cuts to make a sandwich," Peter responded, as he turned around to look at her.

"I'm really hungry, but when I look at you, my appetite has changed to a different kind of hunger as I see how beautiful you look," he continued.

For the moment, she shuddered because of the way he looked at her just like Paul used to. Yes, he was good, real good. He knew all the right things to say. Her head started to spin and she became lightheaded. Her emotions took over. She yearned to be held. Yes, it had been that long.

As he moved closer, he slowly raised his hand and stroked her face gently, and said, "You are so beautiful. How is it that you're left here at home all alone with just me? It feels like it was meant to be," as he started to kiss her tenderly and very slowly on her neck to move eventually to her open lips building up the excitement in her to want it. And, she did.

# Chapter 8

## ~A Huge Mistake~

The heat between the two became irresistible and too hard to handle for her. Carla and Peter began to have frequent secret meetings at the cottage for the next few weeks. Peter knew he had the advantage because he looked just like Paul. The pool man, Nestor, had noticed the strange goings on, but would never say a word out of fear that he would lose his job. He felt very threatened by Peter. After a while, Carla realized she should have her head examined, and felt terribly guilty.

She wanted the attention, but she still loved her husband. But, he was just too busy to notice her. She yearned for his attention. Looking at Peter, reminded her so much of Paul. While Paul's focus was on making more and more money, in his mind he felt he was doing the right thing for her. He didn't realize how he hadn't prioritized their marriage, and how neglected she felt. Success was an addiction for him.

As Carla tried to busy herself away from Peter and the house more, he would comb the town looking for new targets and at times pretended to be Paul. He wasn't very loyal and had no conscience. One night he picked up a local woman, and brought her back home to the cottage. He made sure that Carla heard their banter back and forth to make her jealous. It did, but it, also, infuriated her. She began to reflect on her life since she met and fell in love with her husband. She wondered how she could get rid of this lowlife that she made such a huge mistake with.

The next morning, she went to the cottage to tell Peter it would be best if he moved out, only to find he wasn't there. The door was slightly ajar and opened more as she knocked. It looked as if he had cleaned up the place and packed up.

She caught out of the corner of her eye, a copy of her husband's itinerary in the trash can. She knew Paul had left his itinerary on the kitchen counter when he left. She left it there on purpose, but he made a copy? Or maybe Paul just gave him a copy? It was weird, she thought. She thought it was not only quite odd, but why would he need it? Should she bother and confront him about it later? Would he be back? She had a lot to think about it.

Carla had a few errands to run and didn't want to think about him. She was excited because Paul would finally be home tomorrow. As she got in her car, she saw a note taped to the steering wheel. She was nervous and afraid. She slowly managed to open it carefully as she took a long, deep breath. Peter had written her a goodbye note and thanked her for enriching his life. The letter continued that it was time he moved on because he couldn't handle the guilt of taking his brother's wife, and he wouldn't be able look his brother in the face, anymore.

"How crazy! Who enriched who?" she said aloud, "He had probably found some other poor soul to mooch from." She tore up the letter. She was crazed and overcome with emotions. How could he have put their stupid, meaningless affair on paper? She ripped it up in several pieces and continued on with her day to take her mind off of things. Carla still longed for Paul and became very sad and ashamed of her infidelity. She would've felt much better if she had confronted Peter face-to-face. She had so many things she wanted to tell him in person.

Carla needed to tell him that she was still very much in love with Paul, and what they did was so wrong and that it should never be mentioned again. She knew it was a huge mistake to even trust him for his silence, but it didn't matter now. Hopefully, he was gone for good. He would not be a part of their lives anymore as long as she could help it. It was a relief that he left. Now she hoped to get on with what was left of her life.

She returned from shopping and went back to her last painting. It made her feel very satisfied because it would be of their lovely home. Carla knew it had to be good enough to be hung over the bed in the master bedroom. It truly helped her take her mind off of things that gnawed at her.

Paul would be home soon enough, and she couldn't wait to see him. When Paul called, she told him that Peter had left, but didn't leave a forwarding address.

"Well, that's my brother for you! I had a feeling he was going to take off. The job wasn't working out for him. I knew it was too good to be true. We tried hon. I'll be home soon. I love you and miss you, my sweetness," Paul said with such an endearing tone of love and compassion that she missed. He knew he had neglected her, and he could sense it.

She hadn't heard "sweetness" for a long time, and always did when they made love. She tried not to think about it. That was the only way she could handle it now. Just knowing he would be home soon was all she could think of. She couldn't wait to hold him. Although, his business trips weren't her world, Paul was her world. While she had gone on a few of his trips in the past and was incredibly bored, but now, in her mind, things had changed. Carla would make a great effort to go with him the next time. She would attempt to learn more about his business and express a much greater interest in it. She hoped they could get back on track.

"Honey, I miss you so much and I can't wait to see you," she told him, and sighed.

In the meantime, Peter hadn't left town. He was holed up in some dive motel a few miles away. He had hatched a plan to put in motion and soon. He reviewed it in his mind over and over again. It would change the way anyone would think of him, and it wasn't in a good way. He wanted success, but he didn't want to work too hard for it. He pitied himself and became enraged with jealousy. He always felt like the underdog to his brother and needed to break free of this hatred and the only way to feel relieved of his anguish was revenge.

He was mad and ashamed of himself for not being what his parents had wanted him to be. He didn't know what to do anymore. He was tired of being looked at like a failure. Paul had always been the favored one since they were born. Peter had no desire to work his butt off like Paul. He didn't have the skill set, and he would try to accept that, at the same time it drove him mad with rage.

# Chapter 9

## ~Up To No Good~

Peter called the office very early in the morning, as he pretended to be Paul. He told the secretary, Hildy, to send out messages to all of the office staff involved at the business trip that everything had been wrapped up early, and it was okay to head out and go home. The more important meetings were done and only the voluntary conferences were left to attend, if they wanted to. Although, most did not...

As all the staff got the messages, Paul didn't complain, or ask why. He just thought it was from the higher ups, and he was thrilled to get out of there! Paul deserved a much-needed reprieve and was burnt out. He wanted to go home to his Carla. He had been working too much lately and really wanted to make it up to her. He thought she was too good for him. He realized they had fallen into a rut and he wanted to make some important changes, too. He wanted to remind her over and over how much he loved her. It was a thrill to pack up and leave right away and he would arrive home a day early to surprise her. He had met with all the people he needed to see, so it was a no brainer to cut the trip short.

Peter, on the other hand, continued to scheme. While he knew Paul would arrive home early, he'd find only him around. Unbeknownst to Paul, not only had Peter made the dummy phone call earlier to the office, Peter had just slithered back on the grounds, like the snake he was. Peter had waited for Joanna, Nestor, and Carla to leave. He knew all of their schedules…

Joanna had been out to run some typical errands, while Nestor had been at the local gardening store, and Carla was out getting her hair done. With no one home, and just as Peter had plotted, Paul had arrived home a day early. The car service dropped him off and left. Peter went out to happily greet him.

"Hey, bro! Welcome home!" said Peter.

"Wow, I thought you packed up and left! What's going on?" asked Paul.

Peter, acting all lost and sad, went on about how he came back to talk with him about how he had had a revelation about his life, and that he needed a friendly ear. He told Paul he was ready to go all in and take him back up on the job offer again, and promised he would take it more seriously this time. It was music to Paul's ears. Paul had hoped Peter would come around when he 'woke the heck up!'

It was such a gorgeous day and Peter turned to Paul and said, "Let's take a well-deserved break and get out on the water! We haven't been alone for a long time, or hung out for years, just the two of us to really catch up with no interruptions. What do you say?"

"Sounds good to me, let's go! I really need to unwind!" Paul agreed. "Besides, Carla didn't expect me home until tomorrow. This could help de-stress me totally," he continued.

"C'mon, bro, let's go! We can get some quality time in, and hang out like old times," said Peter.

Peter was quick to help bring in Paul's few bags, and tossed them into the small angular closet under the large staircase. At the same time, Paul went to the kitchen and got the keys for the backyard shed where all the rowboat accessories were. It had a stockpile of oars, cushions, pillows, and tools. Both Paul and Peter continued out the kitchen back door to the end of the property.

"Wait just a minute, I want to make reservations for dinner tonight real quick," Paul said as he turned to go back.

"C'mon we don't want to lose any light. It's so perfect out now. You'll have plenty of time to call when we get back in. Besides it's a weeknight. It won't be crowded," Peter said.

"Yeah, you're right. Okay, let's head out," continued Paul, "This will actually be a lot fun! I'm just so glad to be home."

Peter couldn't wait to put his plan in motion. Not only did he know everyone's schedule, he knew the office staff's itinerary, too! He had too much carte-blanche all over the house, the property, and the office. Plus, as usual, he had Paul eating out of his hands. At first, he didn't have the courage to go through with it, but the timing was too perfect. He felt it was actually too perfect of a plan, not to carry out.

Peter grabbed the rowboat and slid it halfway into the water. Paul had the sturdy oars in hand, while both of them took turns to getting in. Eagerly they went off and drifted out on the water. Peter looked around nervously, and made sure that they were the only ones around. The waters were pleasantly calm, but there was fury in Peter's heart. All he could think when he looked at his brother was that Paul had everything he wanted, while he had nothing. They drifted out further and further and were lucky they had the entire private area to themselves. It was so nice and quiet, and the neighbors lived very far away. You never saw anyone around. As the sun went down, some fog began to roll in as well.

"This is the life," remarked Paul. "We should really do this more often!"

"Yeah, bro, you really have it made," said Peter, with a bit of an attitude.

They talked about old times growing up then it started to get cloudy.

"As peaceful as it is, I guess we should turn back now, though. Before you know it, we won't be able to see well enough," said Paul.

Peter's mind began to race. He started to get cold feet. He didn't know exactly when, or if he was going to act on his dreadful plan, but when Paul turned ever so slightly to grab the oar that slipped out of his hand, Peter just snapped and took the opportunity he needed. He grabbed the heavy wrench hidden under the nearby cushion. It was wrapped in a linen napkin he had grabbed on the way out from the house. He struck Paul on the back of the head and then Paul slumped over. He hit him really hard. Peter checked him, and rushed to take off his wedding ring, watch, and empty his pockets. He pushed his limp body over the side of the boat and watched him disappear under the water.

He quickly rinsed out the linen napkin in the water to get rid of any blood, because he had to bring it back before Joanna would notice it was gone. He didn't want to chance any fingerprints on the wrench with all its grooves, so the napkin was easier to deal with. He threw the wrench to the back of the boat, and quickly rowed back to shore, alone; and, although, he never looked back, he knew Paul was gone.

He planned to row the boat back fast, and then return it to the side of the shed where it was. If anyone asked, he would say he went out by himself. He raced back into the house, rinsed the napkin once more in the sink, threw it in the dryer for a few minutes, and then threw it in the hamper with the regular wash. He ran to take out the luggage from the closet and left them in the foyer as if 'he' had just come home. Soon after, Joanna came in through the side door with several bags of groceries and some dry cleaning. She began to put nearly everything away, prep for dinner, and then she would set the table.

"Darn, I knew I had all those napkins in here somewhere," Joanna said aloud. She noticed everything when it came to all her organized household items.

Peter overheard her from the next room. He just came out of the shower and put on Paul's clothes while he styled his hair like his brother's, too. He, also, remembered to put on his brother's wedding ring and watch.

"Who's there?" asked Joanna. Since she had come in the kitchen's side door, she hadn't seen the luggage in the entry foyer yet.

"It's just me, Joanna. I came back a day early," said Peter, as Paul. "I threw the napkin in the hamper to be washed. I messed it up while I was working outside with it. It happened to be the first thing I grabbed on the way out. I'll buy more if you need," he continued.

"No, that's fine," said Joanna, who thought it was strange. She knew Paul would never do anything stupid like that. He had more class than that. Maybe his dumb brother would, but not him. She went on with her duties and filed her concern in the back of her mind.

"Men, I guess they'll grab whatever they can to fix their toys," she mumbled under her breath.

Peter felt off the hook, and now it was really time to play Paul. Next would be to fool Nestor in the garage. When he saw him, he just waved. He would pass with flying colors. Too easy! He knew Nestor didn't care for small talk or any kind of talk, for that matter. One more left to fool, and then I'm home free, he thought.

Under his breath, "I'm in - not out!"

Just then, Carla came in the front door with a few packages and a beautiful new hairstyle. When she saw Peter as Paul there with the suitcases, she dropped the packages and ran into his arms. She practically knocked him over as she hugged and kissed him all over.

"Perfect timing!" he said.

"What happened? You're a day early, not that I'm complaining, but what a great surprise!" Carla said.

"We finished up early. What do you say we go out for a night on the town?" he asked.

"It sounds like a wonderful idea to go out for a nice, welcome home dinner!" she gushed. Carla was thrilled to have this attention. She was incredibly overwhelmed, and extremely happy he was home. Unfortunately, it still seeped back into her mind how guilty she felt about her indiscretions while looking at Paul, but Paul would make any of her confusion and worry go away.

They had a wonderful evening and later that night they made tender, passionate love. It seemed like it was all new again or maybe because it had been a while. She couldn't imagine what came over him, but she wasn't going to fight it; who cared, she thought, it was wonderful! She was happy to be held by someone who really loved her.

"Aren't you going to call me your sweetness?" she asked while they were still slowly kissing.

"Of course, you know you will always my sweetness," he replied.

# Chapter 10

## ~Getting Carried Away~

The next day at home he hung around as Paul. He didn't go into work, and claimed he was on vacation. He pretended to dive in and read all the latest newspapers, and then get into things that seemed unlikely for him. Carla didn't really care; she was just glad he was home. It was his time to enjoy and relax, she felt. No need to go on a fancy vacation. They'd spend a good deal of time together, as they laughed and canoodled. He told Carla since his last trip was such a huge success; he earned quite a few days off to unwind at home. She had no quarrels with that! She loved the way he moved a little differently, more freely, and more relaxed. It kind of reminded her a little bit of his carefree brother, in a way. Although, she was ecstatic that Paul paid a lot more attention to her, it puzzled her slightly, too. He had always been such a workhorse who always ran into work, at every given moment. She, however, would definitely not complain.

As far as Peter was concerned playing Paul, he knew what he had to

do, and what Carla needed - attention. It was too easy. Peter had Paul
down to a science. His moves, his mannerisms, even the way he wore
his hair and clothes. He even remembered how often he would shave.
He knew his routine from when he left in the morning, and when he
came home at night. After all, they did grow up together, and he knew
all of his idiosyncrasies. Peter wanted his brother's life so badly. For
some time, he had had the chance to study Paul with Carla, but now he
wanted his money, as well. Although, Carla came with the life he took,
he continued to use her to keep up with this charade.

So far, so good. Everything seemed normal for a while, until over
the next several days he had purchased several items, and he became
so carried away. He had bought an array of musical instruments to
decorate the walls with, a few video gaming systems, and some random
camera equipment. Paul didn't play any instruments, so Carla thought
it was an odd fascination, but they did look really nice hanging on the
family room walls as a welcomed change.

However, deliveries would arrive almost every day. It was getting
out of hand! Was Paul having some kind of nervous breakdown? He
would convince Carla they should start to live and enjoy more, to
buy what they want; maybe take a few luxury trips to anywhere and
everywhere. Maybe take music lessons or art classes together to make
up for a lot of lost time for all those years he had been such a workhorse
and had left her alone so often.

It's what Carla wished to hear and longed for. She had missed
her husband for so long, and it was nice to hope their future was on a
positive track. She mentioned to him about having a baby, which on
numerous occasions they had spoke about, but this was not the sort of
topic Peter wanted to discuss, as Paul. He didn't know how Paul felt
about this subject.

"We still have time for that; let's just enjoy us for now," he said
rather convincingly. He was good, but not that good. It was always
Carla who had to tell Paul they should wait. He was baby crazy at one

time. Although a little puzzled, Carla agreed, that they should enjoy themselves now.

While Peter continued to enjoy his new life, a man washed up along the Centre Island beach shoreline, dazed and confused. He had hung on to some old driftwood for some time. It was twilight, and the beach was empty, except for one distraught, young woman. She had come to that spot to drown herself to end her desperate unhappiness, but when she saw the man, she ran to help him. She managed to pull him out of the water and onto the sand.

"Whoa, whoa," she reached to steady him as he lost his balance. Sit here for a few minutes. I'll be right back." She looked around and he just shook his head and motioned it back and forth.

Moments later she returned from her car with a blanket and wrapped it around him. His shivering was uncontrollable and he touched his head winching in pain.

"Wow, that's some lump you have there. I've got to get you to a hospital," she continued.

"No, no, I'll be ok. I just need to rest and warm up."

"My name is Hazel, what's yours?" she asked.

"I don't know," he responded.

She helped him up the beach, and led him to her car. She felt it was her destiny to find him and fate had stepped in. It was incredible to her, because she felt like his angel, when in reality, he was hers... he saved her life, too.

He was very weak and disoriented. Exhausted and dehydrated. He just wanted to rest quietly as he composed himself. She urged him to let her call the police and he continued to beg her not to. She was very concerned about who this stranger was. She didn't know if he was crazy, but, at the same time she didn't feel threatened by him.

Her apartment was not too far and she would bring him there to rest and collect himself. She had some extra men's clothes in her apartment from the last boyfriend who had left just a few days ago, which is why she was so beside herself.

Hazel gave him some iced tea and made him a quick ham and cheese sandwich. Once again, she suggested that someone should look at him or maybe they should go to a local hospital. They could possibly help with his memory loss, and look at his lump. Although, it wasn't bleeding, it was pretty big. Again, he refused. He wouldn't have any part of it now. He just wanted to regain his strength, and come to grips. He had begun to feel more energized after he ate, and was just happy to be alive. His hair was a wet, crazy mess and he had some beard stubble, however, he was still very lucky he had survived for hours and hours in the dark, cold water. He was more bothered that he didn't know who he was.

"I need to call you something. How about Harry?" she asked.

"That's fine. If you think of me as a Harry, I don't mind," he replied.

"I should call the police in case anyone filed a missing person report," she said.

"No, I'm good, like I said, I just need to gain my strength back in a day or so and I'll be out of for your hair," he said. "I should look for a place but I don't have anything on me," as he patted down his pockets.

"Listen, you can stay here until you sort things out." She brought out a pillow and blanket so he could get settled on the couch.

"Thanks, I really appreciate your help," he continued, "I just need to close my eyes for a bit." It was late and he drifted off to sleep on her couch rather quickly. He was so exhausted that he slept through the night, until late morning.

The next day, she questioned him again, but he still had no recollection. She insisted they go to the police station to see if anyone had filed a missing person report. He didn't want to go to the police, because he was confident he'd regain his memory soon. He only would agree to see her doctor.

Unfortunately, there was nothing they could do for him. All his tests came out normal, and the lump had gone down quite a bit, too. He was lucky his skull wasn't fractured because, as the doctor said, he took some hit. He needed time. The doctor wanted to report it to the police, if someone had hit him, but he said he fell.

He got along very well with Hazel; so much so, she was glad to take responsibility for him and his recovery. He seemed so different from anyone she'd known before. Even a bump on the head hadn't changed his nature. She could sense that whoever he was, whatever he had been, he was one of the good guys. As for Paul, his new found batch of interesting clothes fit right into his new surroundings, and looked nothing like the successful stockbroker he'd been.

He regained his strength, but not his memory. He would get occasional flashbacks, but could not make heads or tails out of them. It was really difficult for him, because he didn't know if anyone was searching for him, or where he came from. He was just happy to be alive, and in due time to sort things out.

Hazel was a very pretty, tall girl with brown hair and brown eyes, and she didn't know if he was involved with anyone anywhere. He wasn't concerned with his past, so he continued to stay on with Hazel. They checked the local papers daily to see if there were any reports of missing people, but nothing ever came up. It seemed no one was looking for him and he was fine with it.

Weeks would pass and ultimately, they became very fond of one another. They spent a lot of time together. They shopped together, cooked together, watched TV together, took long walks, etc. He had found comfort and trust with her. He was actually very happy and felt carefree. While Hazel had been very despondent over the loss of her old boyfriend, he was a distant memory now. She had Harry now and she felt happy again.

One night Hazel stood in her kitchen and turned to him and said, "I'm really happy I found you Harry. Unfortunately, it wasn't the best of circumstances for you, but I felt it was meant for us to meet," and she went over to kiss him.

He said, "I appreciate everything you've done for me. You made me very comfortable here and you are a very caring person," and he leaned over to kiss her back.

Those kisses ignited some fireworks between the two of them, and she led him into the bedroom. For the two of them it had been a long time, but "Harry" was a gentleman. He didn't know who he was, or if he had anyone else, but he knew she didn't have anyone. He hesitated a little as she led him to her bedroom. She reassured him - "no strings." Slowly, he continued with her onto the bed.

He began to kiss her on her hand then up her arm with gentle, soft kisses up to her neck, then onto her face. No words are spoken. There were only actions. As he caressed her body, he felt very comfortable to be with her; yet, something was still tugging at him that he couldn't understand. Be that as it may, he was gentle and loving with Hazel, and thoroughly enjoyed being with her.

There were many more nights of passion, as they became closer and inseparable. More time would pass and he still didn't know who he was in his past life, as it was all behind him. He didn't think about it that much anymore. You would think he would want to know!

Harry had less frequent, unexplainable dreams with only a few bursts of flashbacks featuring a large, beachfront property. He couldn't explain it. Maybe it was a vacation he once took. He tried desperately to sort them out when he awoke, but, even his dreams couldn't supply any answers.

Time just went on for him as he hung around Hazel's apartment, but he wasn't happy about just doing nothing. He began to get fidgety. He knew he needed to do something. He continued to read the newspapers and looked at all the job opportunities, but he didn't know what he could do. He found that he mostly enjoyed the business sections. He thought maybe it could offer a clue about who he once was. It started to slowly eat away at him to not to know who he was, even though he and Hazel were happy.

For some reason he was afraid to find out who he was. While his nightly dreams still drove him crazy at times, he knew he had to be patient. The intermittent flashes of a woman's face would come and go, but not long enough for him to retain it. He felt it had to mean something. He just couldn't see the face long enough to recognize her and who she was to him. He had hoped the dreams would stop, but they still would persist for some reason. He felt confident it would eventually work itself out when it was meant to be. Although, he was content with Hazel, he now wondered if it was enough because of the frequent dreams.

# Chapter 11

## ~Piece Of Cake~

Meanwhile, back in Cold Spring Harbor, things between Carla and Peter (playing Paul) started to fizzle in the love department. He was too out of hand with all his impulsive buys on silly unnecessary luxuries; designer clothes, designer jewelry, so much wasted money, period. He'd yell at Joanna and order her around, which Paul never did. But, he didn't care about what she thought, anyway. Nonetheless, Joanna cared very much. She remembered how the twins would behave and act when they were younger, because she practically raised them. Something eerie made her stomach turn. She still couldn't quite get there just yet. Maybe being home too much was getting to Paul?

At dinner, Carla commented under her breath to Joanna about his behavior lately and how he would sometimes remind her of his brother. He overheard it, and felt he'd gone way too crazy and overspent. He had become all caught up in his new found power, but he didn't want to blow his cover. Every day another package would be at the door. Again, he convinced her that she deserved the best of everything and started to kiss her. Meanwhile, most of the stuff was for him and so much for his planning a great trip with Carla. He didn't want to take her anywhere. He was too busy searching the house for more hidden valuables.

"I'm going up to bed. Will you be up soon?" he asked. Joanna close by could still sense something wasn't right and hadn't been for a while now. She didn't say much, but she listened well, and heard everything.

"I'll be up in just a few minutes honey," Carla said.

Carla remained downstairs in the kitchen with Joanna as they reviewed the next week's menu. He rushed upstairs to set up the camcorder he had purchased to videotape their next little tryst. He set it up with a clear view of the bed without detection, in low to little light. He taped over the area where the red recording light would blink, and he carefully placed it on the armoire.

He stood in front of the camera as it recorded, and he removed a cap from his left front tooth. Underneath it was a chipped tooth from a childhood accident which revealed his true identity. It seemed to be the only thing that separated the twins physically. He would proceed to turn the sound off, just in case she would utter the name, Paul. Without a break, he would wait in bed for Carla. He wanted to prove that she was a willful participant. He was confident he had everything figured out.

The next morning, he went into his brother's office for the day and felt quite sure of himself. He had kept up appearances, at least, a few days a week. He would show his face, while everyone else did all the work. He played the role of Paul and dabbled with some business deals as him. He became arrogant and cocky. While he had learned a few things from his brother, he certainly hadn't learned everything, and it showed on occasion. Despite some quizzical expressions between coworkers, he managed to get away with it all the time.

One day there was a power lunch with a few staff members, and other colleagues. Feeling sure of himself, he planned to engage more.

He couldn't screw it up since he was on a roll with his new life. Besides, he studied well and long for the part. Oh, sure he glanced at some of his brother's reports and papers at home and in the office, but he hadn't had years and years of true experience. If only he had applied himself this much to get his own life!

Unbeknownst to him, a photographer from the New York Sun Times came in to take a few publicity shots of the thriving and successful company. When the photographer finished taking the pictures, there would be a few short interviews with a handful of key employees, glad for the distraction. Afterwards, they would get back down to business in the boardroom.

It seemed like clear sailing until a co-worker asked a question about the Haber account and Paul couldn't come up with an answer which was the account known as "his baby." He couldn't fake it or call on Trey, his assistant, who was out sick to help answer. He looked like a deer in the headlights. He commented that Trey had all the latest updates and excused himself saying he felt poorly and coughed. All of the co-workers looked at each other puzzled. They didn't know what to make of his actions. It was totally unlike Paul. He excused himself as he left the room. He told Hildy, on his way out, that he felt ill and left for the rest of the day.

He had to collect himself. He knew he had to get back on track or his cover would be blown. Time to regroup before he lost what he had gained, and worked so hard for. He wondered if his charade was over.

He mumbled to himself on his way home as he tried to convince himself that he had pulled it off. He couldn't wait to open a bottle of Scotch as soon as he got through the door. Paul wasn't much of a Scotch man, but Peter was and he started to drink...a lot. He talked aloud to himself in the library. Joanna could hear him (as always), and would tabulate everything in her mind, again. He so badly wanted to grab a guitar and play it. But he knew he couldn't because Paul had never played a guitar in his life. He second guessed himself until he drifted off to sleep in the chair.

In the meantime, Carla was out with Dee for a late lunch to catch up; which was doing her a world of good, especially to have someone to talk to about the terrible mistake she made months ago. Carla told Dee she felt everything was much better, but in a different sort of way. Even though Paul had become more attentive, the buying frenzies were so unlike Paul, and it freaked her out. There was just something different about him, and she couldn't put her finger on it. He gave her more attention, which was great, but was home a lot more. He often seemed to have given up on his work. She entrusted Dee with her concerns. She was so glad she had someone to confide in about it all, even if it was just to vent.

Several days later, the picture that had been taken at the office appeared in a local NY newspaper. Hazel saw it, and, of course, Peter was the incredible image of "Harry!" She couldn't get over the resemblance! Part of her wanted to rush home and show it to him. He loved reading the paper every day, but she didn't want him to see it. On the other hand, she was ambivalent about revealing her discovery.

Since Hazel worked at the local convenience store, he expected her to bring the paper home for him every day at lunchtime. Should she pretend that she forgot it and he'd be okay with it? She was torn because she didn't want to be without him. If he had someone else in his old life, she felt she could lose him forever. She didn't want to go through that, again. But her conscience won out. She decided she couldn't do that to him and she knew she would feel guilty for it. She had to show him the story. She rushed home to show him the paper and had hoped that this might be a clue he had long hoped for.

"Harry, look!" as she shook the newspaper in front of him.

He looked at it and it all started to come back to him; the boat, the clunk on the head, the cold water, the evening fog, the house, the property, Carla's face, and his jackass brother. Dumbfounded, he stared at the picture and tried to soak it in. He acted very calm in front of Hazel, as his mind spun around and around on overload.

"Hazel, it has nothing to do with me. It's just a dumb coincidence," said Paul, as Harry. But, deep-down, he figured it all out and didn't want to upset her. He needed to absorb it all slowly and comprehend it.

Hazel said, "Look at this guy," as she pointed. "He looks just like you!"

"It's uncanny, but they always say that everybody has a twin somewhere," he replied.

She went back to work disappointed, but relieved.

He wept…

# Chapter 12

## ~Top Secret~

He read the whole article and he knew exactly what his damn brother was up to, and asked himself how could he had been so damn naive? He had always had his brother's back! Always! He knew his brother was lazy, but he was shocked by how far he'd go. It was appalling that his own brother was capable of doing this to him. What if his beautiful Carla was part of it, or was she fooled, too? The thought of her living as his brother's wife made him sick. Oh, how can he think she was part of it. Of course, she wasn't. She would never stop loving him. He prayed she was okay. He no longer wanted to be 'Harry' anymore. He wanted to re-claim himself.

He hired a detective to find out what was going on back home. He would stay 'Harry,' for a while longer, until he could find out more information. He would play it out, until he got to the truth. In the meantime, he would stay on with Hazel.

Back home Carla would wonder why their private intimacy moments felt so mechanical lately. The passion seemed empty. Paul hadn't called her by her nickname anymore like he used to when they made love. She had to remind him from time to time. Carla picked up on a few things, and would often speculate that he had been under more stress from work than usual. Maybe he really needed to work more from home.

Meanwhile, Peter had noticed Carla became more insecure. Honestly, he wondered how she could not tell the difference. He couldn't believe that he and his brother where that similar in every area? Peter felt it was time to take whatever money he could from the credit cards and run. He'd had enough of the charade. He no longer wanted to keep the house, the life, and the wife. He didn't know why he had stayed on as long as he had. He could just tell Carla that it's over between them as husband and wife, or just leave. He no longer wanted to live his brother's life. He had had his fun and was bored now. It was time to go.

The next morning, he came down the stairs in a harried state, acted out of breath, with a small packed overnight bag. He told Carla he had to go on a quick business trip to California.

"Something unexpected came up and I have to handle it personally, and I have to leave right away. It will only be for a few nights, I promise. I'll call you as soon as I land," and rushed towards the door. He always left his itinerary; it was a promise he made many years ago to always do when he traveled.

"What city, what town?" asked a very upset Carla.

"This is a last-minute trip, like I said. I'll be home in a few days, don't worry. I'll call you from the airport as soon as I land if you want," he yelled.

"If I want?" she questioned. "That's alright, I can just call the office for the information," she continued.

"NO!" He screamed, "I mean there's no reason for you to call the office. They're so busy with deadlines and all. I'll call you as soon as I can, I promise! Besides they might not have it on my itinerary yet," and went back and gave her a peck on the cheek goodbye.

"I have to go to San Francisco, that's all! It's a hush-hush thing." (It was the only place he could think of off the top of his head). Carla couldn't believe it. She was truly taken aback. With him being weird and cranky as of late, she began to have doubts about him and the marriage, again. She didn't understand what was going on with him, and why all of a sudden there was such secrecy about this California trip.

After he left, Carla called her mother-in-law, Pat. She asked to see if she had spoken to Paul recently, because he hadn't been himself lately. As they had nothing to report, she was about to hang up, when Pat asked how Peter was doing.

"We haven't heard from him in months," Carla said.

"What? We thought he was still with you!" said Pat and continued, "He called us last week and he said was still there with you. I left him a message just yesterday that a detective named Moe Trotman came around the house looking for him, and gave him your address."

"Well, no, he left and didn't say where he was going. But I have more concerns about Paul," said Carla.

Pat asked, "What concerns about Paul? I wouldn't worry too much about him, Carla. It could be just the stress of the job. Give him more time."

The following day, an older man drove up the long driveway in a beat-up old Dodge and waved to Nestor, "Can I talk to the lady of the house to ask her a few questions?" Nestor pointed to the front door's intercom. Moe parked his car and walked slowly to the front door and pushed the button on the panel. Carla answered and briefly spoke with him. He introduced himself as a magazine writer interested in Paul's successful rise as a businessman in the world of finance. She remembered that Pat had mentioned a detective that expressed an interest in Peter, so she answered carefully.

"Paul just left on a business trip to California and won't be home for a few days. Could you come back then?" She knew he had to be that detective Pat spoke of, or maybe he was trying to protect her in front of her staff?

"I'd like to interview you first, actually. To get the softer side of how he is as a person and husband. It would mean so much to me since I'm on a tight schedule. Could I please come in and speak with you face-to-face. I promise I won't take up much of your time," he said.

"Okay. Nestor can show you in," she explained. She was curious where this was going to go. Nestor would escort him through the front door. Carla, although a bit frazzled, appeared in the foyer to greet him. She said she could only give him a few minutes.

She led him toward the living room. He sat on the couch and began to ask all kinds of questions about Paul, but then segued onto questions about Peter.

Joanna, in the meantime, just out of sight, was very attentive. Joanna acted very busy as she cleaned around. He finished his interview with Carla, and asked if he could call her later, just in case he thought of any other questions.

"Of course," she said. "And, again, my husband should be back in a few days, too," Carla said.

The following day Moe called Carla to stop by again. During his visit he told her the truth, but not the whole truth. He admitted that he was really a detective looking into Peter's disappearance. It was for a concerned family member, and that he had been told not to worry her.

"I knew you really weren't a magazine writer looking for a story. I do talk to my mother-in-law, ya know," said Carla.

"Okay, sorry about that, but I felt it was good to say that, so the staff didn't have to know, or have concern. The trouble is that Peter is missing. And I need to know if you've seen, or heard from him at all lately?" he asked.

"But why come here and ask me all these questions? And, who exactly in the family is looking for him?" quizzed Carla. "When I called the parents, they still thought he was living here, but I told them he left a long time ago," she said. "That's all I know!"

"Where is all your staff?" He in turn asked.

"They're around," responded Carla. His questioning was strategic and was not meant to alarm her. However, she was truthful to say she didn't care if Peter was missing. Moe gave her a curious look, but before he left, he looked around and let it all soak in.

"Can I see the cottage?" he asked. He wanted to inspect Peter's living quarters.

"What? Why?" she asked.

"Just in case there's something in there that might give me some insight," he replied. She brought him over and he saw a few things that could help, but he wasn't ready to share his concerns with Carla.

After he left, Carla went to collect herself in the family room. Flipping on the TV she tried to distract herself from Moe's inquiries. She wondered about who would hire such a guy and who would care that much about Peter? Maybe it was someone from his past, or possibly a debt collector? I'm sure that's what it is. Not my problem she muttered, and turned her attention to the TV.

# Chapter 13

## ~Something Is Amiss~

She made a quick phone call to ask Dee for lunch, only to get her machine. Carla's head was full of worry about why her husband had been so strange these last few weeks. Was he having a breakdown, or was she? And what's with this detective snooping around for Peter?

While Peter as Paul called to keep the peace for now, she still thought it was an odd, short call. He still wouldn't tell her much. He said it was a big surprise and that he would see her in a day, and not to worry. She felt it was so unlike him, and it really bothered her. He had always been honest and open with her.

She decided to call Hildy, Paul's personal secretary. Maybe she would know something by now. Unfortunately, Hildy had no knowledge of his California trip or his whereabouts. Now, all Carla could do was trust him. She told herself it was no big deal that he went away, and he didn't want to tell anyone. She reassured herself that people do it all the time.

In the meantime, Moe came back again and looked around outside for any more clues he may have missed. He asked to see the boat shed in the back. He inspected it well and saw some important clues.

Carla let him do his thing, but right before he got into his car, Carla rushed outside to the driveway and happened to catch him before he left.

"Who hired you to look for Peter?" asked Carla, "I have a right to know!"

"Why, what happened?" Moe asked, seeing how upset and worried she was.

"I just called the office and they told me that Paul was never scheduled to go on a business trip to California and his personal secretary, Hildy, knows everything about his trips. Or, at least, she usually does!" she said. "Maybe it really was a secret trip, so I don't know when he'll be back." She tried to remain calm. She had to look like she had trust in her husband, but Moe saw how upset she was and it didn't surprise him.

"I have some ideas. I can follow up with you tomorrow," Moe said, and drove away like a madman.

"What a jerk! He kind of reminds me of my old bus driver, Cosmo. What is going on here? I know I should call Trey! Of course, he must know something," she said aloud. Paul always confided in Trey, sometimes more than Hildy.

Trey didn't have any answers, either for Carla, but asked, "Was Paul feeling any better? Was he up for the trip he went on?"

Puzzled, she knew Paul hadn't been sick. "Sick?" Carla asked, "When was he sick?"

Trey said, "I heard he left early the other day. He complained he wasn't well."

"Oh, yes, he was better when he left for the trip, thanks," she replied. Carla didn't want to make Paul look bad, just in case there was some kind of logical explanation. She hung up not knowing what to think. Where is he, she wondered. How hush-hush was this trip? Seriously, where did he really go? Was he in some kind of trouble?

She went to the living room, curled up on the sofa and tried to calm down. Confused, she tried to convince herself not to stress out and worry. Of course, she couldn't help it. Something just didn't make sense. She took a deep breath and tried to believe everything would be alright, but her head started to pound. Paul would be back home soon just like he said he would. He had to be. If there was anything wrong, she would have heard.

The more she thought about it, the more she was bothered that there was something strange about Hildy's reaction to her call. While Trey's voice was a bit calmer, he had seemed confused, also. No one knew anything. How could no one know where he went? She considered calling the boss. Then again, she didn't want to get Paul in any trouble. Something was terribly amiss.

Maybe he was having a more serious breakdown than she'd thought! It's been known that this business can be very stressful. She tried to relax more, and stay logical as she wrapped herself up in a comfortable, plush blanket. The more she brewed, the worse she felt. Music could usually soothe her so she put on some easy listening music. She slowly closed her eyes, and then it hit her like a ton of bricks!

"Oh, my God! How could I have been so stupid?" she yelled aloud.

# Chapter 14

## ~A Ton Of Bricks~

She realized why he never whispered her nickname in bed early on, and why she had to always remind him! It was Peter! It had been Peter all along! She felt so violated and disgusted. Especially, since she talked about Peter when she thought he was Paul! All the damn lies! He had her really fooled. She felt sick to her stomach. It began to twist in knots. Where was Paul and now where the hell is Peter? Her head felt heavy. How could she had not known? How stupid she felt! She cried herself to sleep.

Sipping on her morning coffee she sat at the kitchen table looking out. There were too many unanswered questions. Unfortunately, if Moe found anything, he wouldn't divulge any of it to her. It wasn't good that she had given both Joanna and Nestor the day off today. She went to look around the house herself for any clues and then it dawned on her. She ran up the stairs and opened all of Paul's drawers. They had all been rummaged through. She checked the safe and everything was gone except for one small envelope. She began to read it and weep. It was the speech Paul had made when he proposed to her.

A wave of nausea hit her and she ran to the toilet and became really sick. As she came up from her knees, she was hit on her head from behind and lost consciousness. Bound and mouth covered with tape, she was slumped over on an old wooden chair. When she groggily opened her eyes, she tried to focus and realized that she was in the basement. She struggled to move, but she couldn't. Peter had his plan in overdrive and had decided to keep her in a drug induced state so he could tie up some loose ends financially with her.

"Why?" she muttered as she tried to hold her head up.

He wanted to know where the important stock documents were. They were worth millions of dollars. He thought he had found everything but this was the pot of gold he desperately wanted.

"I promise to let you go on the condition you tell me where those papers are, and I will be out of her hair forever. I swear I'll never bother you again," he said.

"What have you done to Paul? Where is he?" she sobbed.

"I don't know. He told me you both weren't cutting it anymore. That things had changed."

"Then why did you take over his life with me?" she questioned.

"He told me I could have you; that he thought you were just another spoiled bitch!"

She began to cry, "He would never say that, never! You're a filthy liar!" she screamed.

"I have to get out of here! Just tell me where they are, and I'll be out of here. But before I go I just want you to watch a little home movie." He had a TV and a VCR set up, and pressed play for her to see the video of the time when they were in bed.

"Oh, my God! I can't believe I slept with the devil himself," she yelled.

"If I get what I want you can have this videotape," mused Peter.

As she tried to compose herself while in disgust, she blurted out, "It's above the very last kitchen cabinet on the right in a fake cabinet front. It slides down and out. There you'll find what you want," she exclaimed.

He placed the tape back over mouth again and then ran up the stairs and found the documents. When he went back down the stairs, he showed her that he found the papers. He bent down as if to untie her, but jabbed her with another needle instead.

Convinced she was out cold; he went back up the stairs again and placed the videotape with the suicide note on the entry foyer table. The note went on to say:

> *I am so sorry I cheated with Peter.*
> *I am so ashamed and have brought disgrace on our family.*
> *This is best for all. Please forgive me.*
> *Goodbye, Carla*

Peter went back downstairs, untied her and carried her limp body up the stairs. He would open the back sliding glass doors to the porch, and check to see if the coast was clear. As usual, all was quiet and he would proceed to carry her out to her car at the back of the property where he had parked it earlier. He would position her in the front seat of her car and then start the engine as it was very close to the water's edge.

"How glorious, my love," Peter said to the still drugged Carla. He felt no one would bother with an autopsy because of the videotape with the suicide note.

Meanwhile, Joanna didn't feel right about having been given more time off. She decided to call Nestor, who happened to live nearby, and asked him to stop in and check to see if Carla was alright. She worried about Carla and that she hadn't looked well yesterday. She felt it wasn't right that they both had the day off.

Nestor said, "I don't mind, I was out buying chemicals for the pool, and was on my way over there, anyway." He had nothing better to do today, and didn't want to leave the chemicals in his truck overnight.

As he parked his truck at Carla and Paul's, he heard a car engine that echoed in the back of the property. How strange, he thought, to hear a car back there. Aware of Joanna's concern, he dropped everything and ran to see what was going on and saw Paul/Peter bent over Carla. Nestor knew right away something was so horribly wrong and grabbed a baseball bat from the backyard and charged at him.

Peter didn't hear Nestor pull up because of Carla's car engine running while the waters thrashed against the shore today. The seagulls screamed above, as if they were angry. Peter was just about to shift the car into drive when Nestor hit him with the bat and knocked him to the ground.

As this was all going on, Dee pulled up and entered the house and called out for Carla. Her concern had taken over because Carla hadn't answered her phone calls when she knew she was home alone. Carla would always return her calls. Through the kitchen windows, Dee saw all the commotion.

Dee called the police immediately as she saw Peter on the ground. Nestor pulled Carla out of the car and shut the ignition off. Peter just lay there, out cold!

Nestor wasn't a youngster, but he really did enough damage to Peter to keep him down as he and Dee revived Carla.

The cops came and Nestor told them what he saw. Peter woke up, and they slapped the cuffs on him. He yelled, "She killed my twin brother! I'm under duress! I don't know what I'm doing." They literally had to drag him away as he kept his insane rant up.

"You're a piece of crap!" Dee yelled.

Moe was called in, because the cops knew he had an active investigation going on with the family, and he had several friends on the force. He told the cops not to let that bum, Peter, bullshit them. Carla was taken away to a hospital in an ambulance and Dee rode along with her. Nestor finally caught his breath and was grateful he was there when he was but he sure didn't fully understand what had happened to Paul.

Moe snuck into the house, and fortunately, he grabbed the videotape with the note and hid them under his baggy coat. Soon after, a few police officers followed in behind him. He knew he could get into a lot of trouble if he took evidence, but felt if the police took it, it would be locked up in the evidence room for a while. Moe had an idea what it was, and he felt Carla had been through enough lately. Right now, what difference would it make?

# Chapter 15

## ~A Short Walk~

Nestor called Joanna, and told her what had happened. Joanna said she would go to the precinct and meet him there soon. She would bring the linen napkin she pretended to wash, but never did. She retrieved the soiled one she had kept, hidden in a plastic bag under her mattress and box spring. All along she felt something wasn't right with "Paul" ever since that day he'd been sharp with her. Paul would never yell at her. In her gut, she felt he was acting more like Peter. Now it all made sense. She had been around for a better part of their childhood to help raise them both. Now that she knew it was Peter all along, she was relieved, but she was still concerned about where Paul was. They all were.

Carla was released from the hospital soon after. Peter would be later denied bail and would stay there until his trial. She wasn't told of his charges yet, but she just ached to go home. It scared her to consider where Paul was. Had Peter hurt Paul? Dee stayed with her for the rest of the evening and then Joanna took over to care for her. They encouraged her to rest and recuperate, yet she still couldn't get over these past events. She spent a lot of time trying to come to grips with all of it.

In the meantime, Moe had filled Paul in on what occurred and how his brother had wanted to take over his life, AND wife. He told him that Carla has been through a lot and he urged him to go easy on her. She had been deceived by Peter and then was attacked by him and had just been released from the hospital. It would take her some time to recover from all of it.

"I had a crazy brother, Cosmo, who used to drive a school bus. He passed away a few years ago, and I finally got the chance to get over there to finish cleaning out his dump. I found a few nice things. He once told me that out of all the kids that were on his bus route for years, there was only one kid that ever gave him a thank you note with a beautiful poem in it. He would cherish that poem 'til the day he died. Your wife was the one who wrote it!" Moe said.

"Wow! She always did love to write, my Carla. I hope she still loves me. What if she can't stand the sight of me because of my brother?"

"Don't worry about that pal. If it's right, you'll know it, so don't sweat it now. You can sweat when you see my bill!" Moe laughed.

Even before Moe's report, Paul had leveled with Hazel. They realized their relationship was better off as just a friendship. Although she was sweet, she was definitely not his Carla. They would part as friends who were there for each other in their time of need. There seemed to be a higher power that had brought them together that fateful night.

Paul was just happy to find out from Moe that Carla would be alright physically, but emotionally it may take some time. He still had a lot to think about. He still couldn't grasp how the love of his life didn't know it was his brother. They couldn't have been that much alike, even in the lovemaking department. He knew how his brother was, but could he ever forgive her, or was it her forgiveness he needed for trusting his brother? Was he to blame that he opened his home to him and told him to help himself to anything?

Moe wanted to tell Carla that Paul was okay and bring him home, but Paul had insisted that he hold off and not share any news about him with her just yet. He had to do it his way when he was ready.

Back home Carla felt strong enough to go for a walk. After all she'd been through; she couldn't get it through her head that she had been so fooled. She felt so stupid and ashamed. Still, she wondered, where was Paul? As Moe continued to work on the case, he promised Carla he would call her with any news. If only...

"Joanna, I'm going for a short a walk," she said.

"Do you want me to come with you, dear?" Joanna asked.

"No, I need to be alone, but thanks, anyway," Carla replied, "but if Moe should call with any news, please come and get me!" Carla continued.

She walked out the back kitchen door toward the water as she had many times before. This time was the first time with a very heavy heart. She wondered what to do now. As she watched the water, she felt a calm come over her. She watched the birds and thought about what an easy life they had. She tried to make sense of it all and wondered how her life had been so messed-up. Even though she had a hard time of it, more-so, could she ever forgive herself?

Although, she had a beautiful home with all of its beauty, it didn't matter. Not without the love of her life. Could Peter have hurt Paul? Where was he?! She had thought she had everything she could ever want, but now, it all meant nothing.

Standing there with the gentle wind caressing her sad, but beautiful face, she tried to breathe in the fresh air and exhale slowly to calm her nerves. She yearned to hear his voice and her special word just once more. She ached for Paul so badly.

"What a mess. If only I could go back in time. Where can you be, my love, will I ever lay eyes on you again?" She sobbed inconsolably as the tears rolled down her cheeks, just then she heard a voice speak from behind her.

"Sweetness, I'm here for you. I'm home, and I'll never leave you again," a familiar voice said. All of a sudden, she turned and her heart felt lifted. They embraced and kissed each other as they held onto one another like never before.

Printed in the USA
CPSIA information can be obtained
at www.ICGtesting.com
LVHW042336160324
774670LV00003B/563